UNDERWATER
FISTFIGHT

Underwater Fistfight © 2016 by Matt Betts

Published by Raw Dog Screaming Press
Bowie, MD

First Edition

Cover illustration: Steven Archer
Cover design: Jennifer Barnes
Book design: Jennifer Barnes

ISBN 978-1-935738-82-4
Library of Congress Control Number: 2016930326

Printed in the United States of America

www.RawDogScreaming.com

UNDERWATER
FISTFIGHT

MATT BETTS

Advance Praise

"Quirky is not only one of my favorite words, but what I also strive to be. In my life and in my musical/TV projects. I'm happy to see someone else out there spreading some good quirk around. But, what strikes me, is that in a fantasy/sci-fi world of Deathbots, zombies, mad scientists and monsters, there can be so many touching, even poignant beats. (Also, something I strive to do in my work.)

"Serve up your quirky with a side of heart and soul. It's not an easy path to walk. Pee Wee did it, The Shazzbots do it, and so does this book. Trust me, I would know, I'm a Space Captain. Underwater Fistfight... Come for the Deathbots, stay for the feels."

—Ian "CAPTAIN CAPTAIN" Hummel, The Shazzbots

"Betts' poetry lures you closer with its quirkiness and whimsy and then delivers a dark and bewildering insight on the world, on death, on life, on murder and uncertainty. It is oddly like walking along in an amusement park and finding yourself alone in a dark room with only your thoughts and fears. Yet, as unsettling as that might be I found myself coming back for more."

—Leslie J. Anderson, *An Inheritance of Stone*

"Every time I open this book, I re-read various passages in new and different lights; I purposely like to thumb through when I'm in different moods, to experience Betts' situational objectivity through a variety of landscapes—underwater fistfight indeed! This isn't a must-read; it's a must-read-over-and-over."

—Jerry Macaluso, Effects Designer (Toxic Avenger II&III), Producer (Night Skies) and Founder of Pop Culture Shock Collectibles, Inc.

Contents

Thanks to:

All of the friends who got me interested in speculative poetry. There's a big list.

Big hugs and thanks to:

My family: Kenz, Calvin, Miles, Mom and Dad

Educational Supplemental #36

The Origins and Terminology of Modern Poetry

So, poetry. It's a lot to take in. Am I right?

Let me explain it to you.

You may have noticed a good many nautical terms when studying poetry. This is due to the heavy influence of pirates on the art form. Once you understand that fact, it's much easier to understand on so many levels.

Want to say something, but not really mean it? This is known as a metaphor, or Punching the Shark. Calico Jack is believed to have introduced it when he said "Arrr. This shark be death."

Can you rhyme three words in a stanza? That's a Seaweed Surprise. Rare. Blackbeard mastered that one.

Repetition is a powerful weapon in any poet's arsenal. "Yo, ho, ho" is a famous example that most children learn in school. Captain Kidd was a student of the repetitive school. In fact, he coined the phrase "Yo, ho, ho, HO." Adding the extra 'HO' in order to get his point across.

A simile is when you compare one thing to another, using the words "like" or "and". Red Legs Greaves was mocked for this technique which was known as the Trident Full of Chum before it caught on.

But poetry as a whole? Expressing feelings, emotions? Pirate/poets call that the Underwater Fistfight. Don't be confused with similar terms, like

Full Fathom Fisticuffs or Undersea Shenanigans, because that kind of talk belongs in the brothels.

No, the Underwater Fistfight is the eternal struggle to attach meaning to our existence. For as long as there have been pirates, poets have been Stabbing the Orca with a Full Sail, Eating the Bobbing Mackerel, and Pouring Grog into their Muskets. Sure, sometimes they got Parrot Bubbles and occasionally, the Sunset Smelled like a Giggling Albatross, but once in a great while, readers got a real Cutlass to the Eyehole. Literally.

They *were* pirates after all.

12th Night of the Living Dead

Romeo turned out to be less complex
than Juliet thought;
Wore his heart on his sleeve,
someone else's spleen on his trousers.

Hamlet was less melancholy
once he understood
that he was the thing
rotten in the state of Denmark.

Lady Macbeth spent her days
hungrily lapping blood
off her hands—
those damned crimson spots never drying.

Almost See the Bottom

I'll wait right here on the dock with a lantern.
Watch the bay for your return.
The sea air would do me good.

Or I could sit on your back porch until you come drifting home.
Wrap myself in a tattered blanket
to keep warm.

You can't hide forever. Not at sea.
Not behind *that*, or any other monster.

I should stand at the trail head that forks on your morning walk.
The one where you always decide
to go right instead of left.

I am that left trail you never decide to choose, aren't I?
You stare hard at me for a moment.
And choose the safe route.

That monster of yours is enormous.
Big enough to blot the sun
Big enough to move mountains

But I still see you.
And I know...
You can still see me.

An Imbalance of Humors

That stuff all over the news?
War, murder?
Shooting, stabbing?
Kicking, screaming?
None of that gives you pause.

You've made your peace with
Crazy neighbors, terrorists,
Cultists and clowns.
The random lunatic
With an axe to grind and an axe to swing

The fringe stuff?
Black-eyed children at your door,
UFOS, Bigfoot?
Chupacabras and lake monsters?
Yawn.

As they've told you from birth,
It's what's inside that counts:
That tingle in your arm?
Maybe it just fell asleep.
Or maybe it's a nest
of spiders hatching
just
beneath
the surface
of your skin.

That last taco you ate might
be what is making your

stomach rumble, but the sloshing
sounds more like
an oversized leech,
doing some laps,
making
itself
stronger and
tougher.

Is *that* tiny creature the thing you hear
marching in your head?
That sound of a thousand softly
padding feet all in step
The moment you close your eyes?

You never had migraines until you
Moved into that new job. Maybe it's
stress, or maybe the worm you
ate in third grade has finally come
to maturation and it
wants out…
In the
worst
possible
way.

That cough has been lingering.
A little cold?
Allergies, maybe?
Why does it feel like the phlegm is
moving up your esophagus
all by itself?
Like a slug,
ascending

the garden
path.

Is that the same *thing* you hear
mock-stomping in your head?
That sound of a million
bare feet on sand,
the moment you close your eyes?

No, no. Home invaders and
road-ragers?
You can see them coming.
They don't make your
spine tighten and your jaw ache

Like the prickly
blackness
that claws around within your own body,
your head and your heart…
Itching to make its way out.

Another Seaweed Beast, Another Show

1

Codium fragile, is known by many names: Green Sea Fingers, Sputnik Weed, Green Fleece, Velvet Horn, but most ominously as Dead Man's Fingers. It's an invasive, alien type of seaweed. It is known to some as the secret to keeping skin young and supple, and it grows fast in low light. They call it the Oyster Thief because it attaches itself to clams and other things on the sea floor and carries them away when uprooted.

2

"Seaweed Nightmare"

Eustace Daily News—letters to the editor June 23, 1978—Eustace, Texas

I still cannot believe the state of Eustace Park. Little has been done to improve its condition since Hurricane Debra back in '59. You can't access the surf-side water because of the massive amounts of seaweed. It's just completely unpassable. My kids don't even want to go down there because of the Dead Man's Fingers that wash up on the shore, and I certainly don't want them playing with, or around, such filth. I don't like them even picking up anyone's digits, that's for sure. This area hasn't been regularly maintained in some time. The smell is unbearable—like rotting vegetables—and the cloud of flies is sickening. It is terrible all through the beach area. This used to be a wonderful area, but not anymore. Let's bring some pride back to our coastline and clean up Eustace Park.

-Laverne P.-

3

Raw Wakame seaweed has 4 calories per 10 gram serving and has no cholesterol. Dead Man's Fingers can be easily added to casseroles and stews without your even noticing!

4

Dead Man's Fingers enveloped our beloved vessel, threatening to pull it down to the depths of the ocean. That Seaweed Beast tightened its grip and dragged us deeper.

Crushing.

Crushing.

...as Deathbots and Taxes

I
Everyone has a Deathbot following them
waiting for the perfect moment
and time
to fulfill its mission.

There's one in the dark alley
between the flower shop
and pharmacy
on the way home.

Two-by-two they hide behind
lamp posts along the path
the neighbors
jog down every day.

A shiny gleaming Deathbot
crouches behind a Volvo
right this very moment in the mall
parking lot.

II
Give yours a wacky name
when you say goodnight.
Bobo, Freckles, Hop-a-long,
whatever puts you at ease.

Then, in the half-light
of the moon,
curl up with
your favorite blanket

and watch the unblinking
red eye
scan you methodically
until you're lulled to a deep sleep.

Blow up Half the World

"I am become death, destroyer of worlds." — *J. Robert Oppenheimer's interpretation of the Bhagavad Gita in describing the atomic bomb*

You have but fitted a loose collar and flimsy leash upon the darkness that unfolds before you.

I shall rise again, wrapped in a thick coat of Oleander.

"I am all-powerful Time which destroys all things, and I have come here to slay these men. Even if thou doest not fight, all the warriors facing thee shall die."

From the Bhagavad Gita

Broken Bodies

The Mutter Museum doesn't allow photographs or videos of their collection, so really it's the perfect place for a clandestine make-out session. No judgment. No paparazzi. No troublesome tourists and telltale images.

My heart.
My breath.

Meet me here in the basement by the stomachs and the stones. And we will make passionate love, your perfect hands wrapped round my back. No one to watch but the wall of skulls on the upper level.

My mind.
My word.

Say yes. The prying eyes of the dead and deformed no longer know pride or hatred. Their sour limbs entwined, they know no means to make us ashamed in our passion.

My blood.
My bones.

The plaster casts of conjoined twins and molds of diseased eyes won't blink or blush upon seeing us. Let me brush your hair back behind your ear, linger gently there against the cold glass cabinets, nose-to-nose with faces bent from turmoil and nature's poor favor.

My my.
My my.

When we gain our composure and part our ways, avert your gaze from the preserved penis and the syphilitic samples on display by the exit sign. Our love will never crumble, never die, never be held up to scrutiny like some common cracked spine or yellowed bone marrow.

My sighs.
My sighs.

Call This River Big Silty

Music is so much better on wax. I love the sound of the needle hitting the record, that soft scratch just before the music begins. But I can't have a record player on the ship. The rocking with the waves makes the song skip far too frequently. It's maddening for a music aficionado, so I don't even try anymore.

There's a track on Herbie Hancock's album *Head Hunters* called Chameleon. I've been a merchant marine, a navy man. I've worked an oil patch outside of Lubbock. Sold medical instruments in Chicago for a time. My brother and I chased demons for the church, and burned vampire terrorists for the government. Down in the islands, I single-handedly drove a zombie army into the sea. There aren't many things I haven't been.

And that's the thing about Chameleon. Its different hues depend on when you listen to it. Where you are. It can be the theme to your favorite cop show, or a serious meditation on the nature of rhythm. Now, as I'm remembering it in my head, I'm only hearing the repetitive bass line walking up the scale. The song sounds complex, yet is deceptively simple, built basically on two chords. Hancock stays on that track for a good fifteen minutes or more.

There is no reason to ever over-complicate things. Music or otherwise. Once they get tied up and twisted, it's time to move on.

Camping Out

Flat on our backs, we let the world go on around us

The hastily built fire added a crackle to keep time with the chirping song
of the night insects

Embers rose into the air haphazardly and fell into the earth
slowly spiraling to the ground like fireflies on Benzedrine.

The trees formed the ceiling of our own private Sistine Chapel
with a moon roof to let the stars shine through.

Content and safe, we fell asleep dreaming of being everywhere else.

The Coming Extinction

Mom loves ELVIS. "Never be another one like ELVIS again," she says. "He was the King." She watches old movies starring him on DVD and shows me websites about him on the Internet. Almost everything about him is in black and white, which proves it happened a long time ago. I saw *Jurassic Park* the other night on the Superstation and it was in color. I think if they can clone dinosaurs and bring them back to life, they could probably bring back ELVIS. In fact, I don't see what would prevent them from bringing back herds of ELVISES to roam free in the wild, tearing across the plains and spitting poison on unsuspecting townsfolk. The news cycle would be filled with footage of them gyrating their hips, curling their lips, and crooning through the heartland of America. It could happen. Anything could happen. Mom says if an ELVIS impersonator comes to the county fair this year, we'll go see him. I hope we sit way in the back of the bandstand. Just in case.

A Contract on Myself

I stood at my bedside and looked down at myself. It seemed like a good way to end it. I could just hold the pillow over my face until I stopped struggling.

I decided I couldn't do knives. The blood would be too much. I suppose at the bus stop I could sneak up behind me with a revolver. Easy enough. Stick the gun up to my temple. Splatter my brains all over the shelter and horrify my fellow commuters. As long as I didn't have to look myself in the eyes when I did it.

It would be so simple to break into my house and poison my Corn Flakes while I was at work. I eat them every morning; I know that. Breakfast is the most important meal of the day.

I fluffed the pillow as quietly as I could. On the bed, it looked as if I was dreaming. My eyes were quivering, mouth moving a little. I was probably imagining I was running in a field or flying along a beach. My legs twitched under the covers, like when a dog dreams it's chasing a car in its sleep.

Ugh. So. Darn. Cute. I can't stay mad at me.

Ooo. I wonder if I could run myself over with a car? How hard would that be? I'd have to time it just right, but I could easily make that look like an accident.

The Crow's Wife

...says "caw" in an accent so thick that the crane waitress doesn't quite understand. "Cow? Did you say you want to order a cow?" The bemused server asks. The Crow's Wife turns red. She's only been married for a week and in the country for a tiny bit longer. She knows she needs to listen to more locals and practice the language harder. The pierced and spiky chicks at the bar look up from their cell phones just long enough to sneer at the out-of-towner.

"No. My husband will be joining me for dinner soon. I'll just wait for him." She pulls her feathers tighter around her shoulders and slumps back into the red leather-encased seat. It was cold so close to the door.

The waitress tries again: "Can I get you a beer while you wait?"

The Crow's Wife shakes her head. "I can't drink. I'm a mynah." She smiles expectantly, but the server just closes her notepad and walks away. The old hens in the corner booth cackle condescension, the humor in their voices not quite the reaction the Crow's Wife was hoping for.

"A crow's coming? Get ready for rain." The bartender tells the waitress with the skinny legs. "And hide your shiny objects." The whole room guffaws and giggles.

In her seat, the Crow's Wife quietly practices her vocal exercises; devoicing sounds and feeling her vocal chords vibrate with the consonants. "Caaawww... Caaaw... Caw."

Desperate Monsters Turn to Spamming

(Don't open emails with these subject lines)

1. Cheap Island Adventure Vacations from Moreau Travel

2. Greetings! My Dark Lord Master decrees you have won the British Lottery!

3. Ever want to be someone else? I have a potion for that!

4. How does immortality sound to you?

5. Deals Good! Fire bad.

6. Never have too much blood again!

7. 10 tips for making your brain fatter and more delicious

8. Beautiful women are hiding under your bed right now! Come see!

9. Want a beautiful head of hair? How about two? Or more?

10. Greetings from the deep dark woods! We have cookies!

Do you hear some kind of song?

I never hear music.
Not from the surface.
This deep,
I hear the songs of the
whales thundering through the
deep sea canyons.
I hear the high pitches of the
dolphins
flitting along the surface.
Down low, the angelfish
make their own melody
crunching coral
in rhythm to their
tiny destinies.

Don't Go Too Far

Let's get mean. Make it
a real fight.—Stabbing,
kicking, spitting.
Got a gun? No?
That's too bad.
I want to get bloody,
Vicious.

There has to be a weapon,
What's in easy reach?
Sharp rocks? Broken glass?
Come on, let's go
at it.
Let's god damn fight.
Rumble.

Are you slapping me?
What's that? Close up your
fist, throw a punch.
I've heard you roar.
You're a big beast.
Stop pushing and waving your arms
Let's rumble.

Enough roaring. Enough. Fight
me, you big freak.
Claws, tails, whips,
whatever. I wanna tear your
insides out.

I want… Seriously. Stop waving your arms.
This is silly. You're silly.

I'm… I'm leaving.

The Long-Term Effects of Auroral Kilometric Radiation on the Earth's Population

The Scientists announced that the Earth screams.
Its cries created high over the planet by particles and magnetic fields.

The nerve-wracking sound—a clatter of whistles and clicks
more powerful than we mere humans could ever generate.

Some suggest that anyone listening out in the stars could hear
since the noise shoots off into space as a concentrated beam.

How funny would it be, if instead of green-skinned bug-eyed aliens
landing at our doorstep to greet us and shower us with technology,

Mars and Jupiter start inching toward us year by year, emitting signals
of their own, translatable by The Scientists only as menace or concern?

Equal Footing

My arms aren't getting any longer
or anything.
They're T-rex stubby.
Look at them. They're useless.

What can *you* do?
No really, what can you do?
One of us has to change.
Right?
Can you stretch your arms
like a rubber man,
inflate your body
like a startled blowfish?

I can breathe fire,
fry things with
heat vision.
Whip-crack with my mighty tail.
I'd be glad to stop any
number of those things
if you think it will help
us become equals.

What can you do?
No really, what can you do?
One of us has to change.
Right?
Can you blast cones of
cold air,

move rocks with your
more-than-mortal mind?

So far, I'm doing all the work
all the fighting
all the saving
all the roaring.
It has to be a two-way street,
a partnership.
There are times when I
need rescued.
Moments when I feel
vulnerable.

Where's my distress call, my little red button?

Failed TV Pilots Featuring Deathbots

1. Little Deathbot on the Prairie
2. Deathbot of Fortune
3. I Dream of Deathbot
4. The Courtship of Eddie's Deathbot
5. The Fresh Deathbot of Bel-Air
6. Welcome Back, Deathbot
7. Married… with Deathbots
8. My Two Deathbots
9. Deathbot, M.D.
10. Chico and the Deathbot
11. Deathbot Dance Party U.S.A.
12. The Misadventures of Sheriff Deathbot

Fear of Dead Celebrities

What other earthly reason would there be
to find *Under Seige 2: Dark Territory*
on at the same time as *Hard to Kill*
or *The Foreigner*?

Has something happened?
Was there an accident?
Did Segal succumb to some terrible
illness, or did a crazed fan go too far?

Coincidences abound.

Is there no other reason than mere chance
that *Gone in 60 Seconds*
battles the airwaves
against *Ghost Rider* and *National Treasure*?

Surely Nicholas Cage is fine.
Surely his cry of *"Let's ride!"*
isn't someone in programming's way
of saying goodbye.

Happenstance is no reason to panic.

The chance to flip between
Catwoman, Swordfish and *X-3: The Last Stand*
should be a time to celebrate Halle Berry,
not to mourn.

Five Questions for the Angel of Death as I'm Taken to My Final Reward

1) How did you hear about me? Check one:
   ❏ Previous customer
   ❏ Internet (specify site below)
   ❏ Word of Mouth
   ❏ Advertisement

2) Would you tell your friends about your experience with me? If another Angel were to come to collect me, would you recommend the experience? If not, why?

3) What have others done better than I have? How could I have improved your experience with me?

4) What made you decide to end my life today? Please be specific.

(Optional) What font do you use on your business cards? Do you go for something classic like Times New Roman, or something more position-appropriate, like gothic or script?

┌───┐
│ Please include additional information in this box if needed. │
│   │
│   │
│   │
│   │
└───┘

Footnotes Are the New Titles

Last year,
Blue was the new Red
Forty was the new Thirty
Pork was the new Chicken

This year,
Plastic is the new Paper
Amused is the new Ecstatic

Up is the new Down
Yes is the new No

Money is the new Time
Gaseous is the new Solid

Soon[1,]
Boy will be the new Man
Tomorrow will be the new Today
We will be the new They

[1]Please mark your calendar

For a Swim

We've never been much for conversation. None of the crew. We're more for action than words, really. Bonding with a stranger comes slow, if at all. But a dip in the harbor is a simple thing. A playful splash, a cannonball off the dock. It's like I'm home in Fayetteville. A child again, with schoolboy friends and schoolboy innocence.

The cool, crisp water drips down my neck.
The cool, crisp water slips slowly down my cheek.
And we're here. With the taunts and the jibes of friends.
And we're here. Mathematics and formulas forgotten
in the current of the river and the stream of time.

Of course, up on the boat, the gray abomination on the deck, that monstrosity that we had the misfortune of saving, assures me that I am not at home. We should have left him in the muck and mire. Should've let the vultures pick his helpless bones clean. But he is with us now. A talisman and an albatross. We must continue. There is no safety here in this water, this foreign heat. We are not all classmates out to cool off. There are monsters here. And horrors never imagined lurking just below the surface.

But the azure river all around and a chance for a swim can't be ignored.

Ghost of a Beloved Children's Show Host

Late nights are the worst;
whispered introductions to
cartoons long forgotten,
nursery rhymes
in low, throaty growls.

He appears as a haze
on the stairs. His long tail
dragging behind, falling down
each step.

Thump
Thump
Thump

Everyone suggests an exorcism
to cleanse the house,
drive out the spirit, bring peace.

But we can't seem to do it.
Just can't bring ourselves to
tell him to leave.

He taught us to tie our shoes
eat our veggies and share.
Showed us how to make
egg carton Thanksgiving
decorations and cotton ball
Santas.

But *that laugh*.
That childish chortle
so jubilant and vibrant in life
now dripping and maniacal.
That happy dance,
hopping foot to foot
seems more of a taunt -
like he's daring us to
chase him out.

Still, he taught us important things
like how to spell the words
'Sad', 'Mad' and 'Go'.
And showed us it's all right to cry.

Going Green with your Deathbot

Hand-cranking your Deathbot is environmentally friendly,
though tiresome and impractical.
It makes for unpredictable results when you order
your Deathbot to carry out elaborate assassinations.

Windmills make your Deathbot top-heavy,
prone to tipping over at crucial moments.
This renders you vulnerable and weak
in the eyes of those who would do you harm.

Hydroelectric power is pretty much out, unless
you own an amphibious Deathbot model A-63.
In that case, an unstable power supply
is the least of your troubles.

If you live in Alaska, should you really replace your
Deathbot's fission reactor with solar power?
The nights get long, the battery
holds only so much, and your enemies are many.

The Golden Age of Railroad Advertising
(Innovations in Love Note Delivery)

It says 'I Love Helen' in five-foot letters spray-painted white across the rounded side of the tanker car. The rest of the train suffers a similar, though more drastic fate - huge block letters of varying colors, obscene pictures and grandiose braggings, some barely legible, others planned and polished.

The graffiti becomes a picture show—a cartoon—a strip of Sunday funnies to peruse while watching the train zip past. The bold words 'I Love Helen' blend with the rhythm of the train; *IloveHelenIloveHelen*.

What better way to declare one's love for another than the blank canvas of a black container of petroleum? Poetry, love letters, flowers are all well and good, but they can be ignored, can be discarded, can be left in a waiting room or dropped in a drawer. Trains however, *Go Places*. They force people to stop and understand The Glory That is Helen and the certainty of one person's love for her whether they want to or not.

As rail cars full of SUVs and extended cab trucks whistle past followed by empty flatbeds and darkened box cars, the question arises as to what the drivers see on the other side of the train? Do they know of this wondrous creature called Helen? Or do they get the garden-variety scribblings and dirty words?

Maybe Helen has, on the other side, reciprocated the love of the unknown admirer with a statement of her own. Or tragically, declared her love for another. Worse still, maybe Helen never got stuck at a railroad crossing and will never know someone loves her. Regardless, the message is moving westward with haste, and by tomorrow will be in Chicago, St. Louis or Birmingham.

Graveyard of Lost Ships

That could be us.
A ship run aground.
Dashed on the rocks
with a split hull swallowing water.

So easy to lose our way
out on the open sea.
We have maps,
we have a compass.

But it just takes one
miscalculation.
An instance of poor
judgement.
A single mistaken star
and it's all gone.

I've watched your hand
on the wheel, guiding us
and I'm afraid
to take my turn at the helm.

The Heart of an Extinct Volcano

There's a girl behind the bar in the hotel lounge. Dark hair, tattoo of maybe a dragon on her neck, maybe a two-headed snake. The man at the piano is letting The Eagles have it with an ambivalence that belies the hour. This is yesterday, and before that, and before that.

The three other men in the place are huddled around a table with a dying candle, talking low about the white man with the beard. They grin. Their tone assumes I don't speak their language. This is last week, and before that, and before that.

On my table, there is a drink with bright colored syrups making their way down the inside of the glass. It is a local concoction of some infamy. One that knocks cocky tourists on their asses. I'm not here to see the sights. This is a month ago, and before that, and before that.

The floor is wobbly but I make my way to the mocking trio. Yes, the outsider knows your words. Unsteady on my feet. Unsteady on my feet. I blow out their flickering candle. This is last year, and before that, and before that.

Hit Bottom

Terrestrial North Pole, all ahead full.
Euler was right, it's a moving target
on a wobbly axis. Still the dream of snowy perfection persists.
(have you heard about the North Pole? North Pole. I hear it's wonderful)

Here's the bearing and here's our course,
but before you lay your hand on the throttle,
and race into the fray,
I have to give you my declination.

I can't be your compass needle,
repulsion and attraction all at once,
spinning.

We can blame the monsters, we can blame the sea,
call upon the gods and curse their names.
(stupid creatures! it's all your fault! Oh the sea, don't get me started)

We've all got our excuses,
but that doesn't change our basic physics,
doesn't alter the lines of flux,
we're still dizzy from forces we can't control.

So let's full ahead to the pole. Follow the sea,
keep our hands to ourselves, arms folded,
eyes on the horizon.
(oh look, a dolphin, a whale, a gorgeous sunset)

So when we get to the north country fair,
where the winds hit heavy on the borderline,

remember me to one who lives there,
for she once was a true north of mine.

I Left My Heart in San Francisco. I Left Yours Somewhere in Colorado...

…or was it Nevada? Hard to say. I travel a lot. And I'm forgetful.

I know I left your ring finger at a rest stop outside of Dallas. But that's only because it was on the news.

Your right ear is still on the washing machine downstairs. I found it in my pants pocket just as I was throwing my jeans into the wash. That would've been embarrassing. All my clothes would've turned out all EAR-colored, *right?*

Shoved your spleen down a sewer grate in Livonia, Michigan. Kicked your jawbone into rush-hour traffic on the Miracle Mile. Wasn't chasing that down, let me tell you. I'm sure it was ground to powder by the time those maniac drivers were done.

It wasn't Kansas City, was it? Where I left your heart? No. I think that's where I left those fingernail clippings. I could take notes, I guess. But really? More evidence?

What was I looking for? Your heart. Right.

Remind me which one is the "Show-Me-State" again?

Ideal childhood

It seemed the sun shone every day
I don't remember rain
    Or snow
    Or blistering heat

I only remember gentle breezes
That tickled my neck
    And raised pretty girls' skirts
    Ever so slightly

As they walked away.

Just a Legend, I'm Afraid

(Three Dreams about Water)

1) *Sometime after falling in love for the first time:* Simple. To the point. I am walking down a long, brown wooden pier. I am hand-in-hand with my high school sweetheart. We walk for a long time laughing and watching the waves break, the sun descending over the water. When we get to the end, we stop and look for a moment. We marvel at the glory of the sea. Then she pushes me in. I wake up with the crash of the waves still in my head.

2) *18 days after getting scuba diving certification:* My friends are goading me. Trying to convince me to do what they are too frightened to. I am climbing the fifty foot mast of a sailboat, hand over hand, until I reach the top. I look down at the boat and feel the sway as the boat rises and falls with the waves. Back and forth. Slightly up. A little down. I gather my courage and wait for the boat to sway the way I think it should be. With the cheers still coming from my friends down on the deck, I leap. The fall goes in slow motion and I have time to fear that the boat will rock back and I will fall onto the deck. It doesn't. I hit the water hard—sinking fast. My buoyancy halts my descent and I hang there in the water, neither sinking nor floating upward. A grape in gelatin. The water is dark. I realize that I don't know which way is up. I release some water from my mouth to see which way the bubbles go, but they cling to my body. I spin myself in circles but I can't decide which way is up.

3) *Out of the blue:* Underwater. Swimming through what seems to be the hold of a sunken cargo ship. There is debris motionless everywhere. Wood from broken crates, cloth and twisted metal. And oranges. Oranges everywhere. There are oranges suspended in the water and I have to push them aside as I swim. I am looking for an exit and swim down a hallway. As I get nearly halfway down, I am passed by the captain of the ship…who is swimming

the other way. I swim further, and the hall quickly narrows to the point where I cannot turn around. Eventually, the passage ends in a tiny door too small to get through. I open it to see what's inside but awaken before I can see it. I wake with the taste of tangerines lingering on my tongue.

The Last History

I don't think I can go to New York another time. Too many ghosts, too many specters in the streets. I'm staying off of 42nd and I'm swearing off Canal.

Crossing London off my list. Maybe Cairo has to go, too. I'm nixing Beijing, Tampa and Nimes. The shadows in the streets make me think too much.

I don't want to give up on Mexico City just yet. I'd miss the churros and chocolate, the smell of the Honeysuckle Market filling my mind.

Certainly can't go back to Inverness. Scotland is rife with spirits. What is this apparition I see before me? "Come, let me clutch thee. I have thee not, and yet I see thee still."

I could just roam the oceans. Walking on water, feet atop the waves. Startled sailors and concerned fishermen be damned.

It would be easy to drift the alleys of Madrid until I lose the sun. Dance in the fountains. Lose my way. Drink Tinto de Veranos until the demons stop dancing in the open doors.

The Lightning Came from Under the Sea

… in a flash of color. In a pulse of electrical discharge. Everything is back-to-front and all confused.

We're all waiting. Waiting for it to be set right.

It could be a metaphor. It could be a phenomenon we need to pull apart and diagram like a compound sentence. Maybe it needs some modifiers to help us figure it out.

The crazy lightning came from far under the deep blue sea.

… in a squiggly indirect path across the gray night sky.

We're all waiting. Waiting for it to end.

Maybe it needs to appeal to the senses before we can make sense of it.

The lightning came from under the sea…

… in a rumble of noise. In a snap of sound. The smell of burning air in the wake of it. The lightning tasted like scrambled eggs and sour milk.

But we're all waiting. Waiting for it to make sense.

I Think He's Looking for Something

Cannons in the streets?
That's nothing new.
Flame throwers reaching red fingers out to me?
I'm used to that.
Panic and terror from the tiny people?
I know too well.

How many times have I wandered ashore
ankle-deep in some poor town's harbor,
head held high? How many times have I
touched the beach, my heart
pounding anew? This could be the day.

I could be the hero.

Stones and sticks airborne at my legs?
I've felt that.
Words, Words, Words?
My ears are full of them.
The blows of hatred?
I know too well.

Maintain Radio Contact

The adults are on a mission and I stare at
the radio. All those dials and knobs. The
readouts that jump and bounce, but all
I hear is static. That fuzzy white noise
that says nothing is good,
nothing is bad.

One flip of the switch
I could be blaring Billy Joel or
Bob Seger in these headphones.
No one would be the wiser.
I have KISS live on reel to reel.

But the static… it's a rhythm
all its own. I can hear voices
in that blizzard of nothing. They're
voices I shouldn't hear.
They reach from the void
with whispers and growls
that tell me to do things—things
that contradict
everything
proper.

Maybe Waldo Had Syphilis

I never found him. I looked. I did. Hours spent with a magnifying glass in one hand, a Sunny D in the other. Scouring faces, following his trail. It just wasn't my thing. Eventually, I gave up. Now that I'm older, I feel bad about it. I mean, what if Waldo was gravely ill and he didn't even know it. The whole purpose of the game might have been to locate him so a crack medical team could get him life-saving medication. Presumably, he's dead now. If my success was any indication.

But you know, thinking about it, maybe that emergency medicine thing was a ruse. It sounds like an excuse mobsters would use in order to get me to lead them right to Waldo so they could deliver him a gruesome fate. Did he owe them money because of a terrible gambling problem? Was it a love triangle? I could see a guy like Waldo sleeping with a gangster's girlfriend. Unknowingly, of course.

I'm glad I didn't find him. Maybe he escaped with the young lady and they're living an honest life in Chicago or Orlando or Vegas. If I know Waldo, it's someplace crowded. He probably works in a mall or a fish market, an airport, maybe. Sounds like a decent life.

Unless... Maybe the criminals already got to him? Maybe that's why I couldn't find him in the first place? Dear God.

Suppose, finally, that Waldo was just an ass with no regard for anyone else's feelings. Suppose that he ran and ran for fun. Keeping one step ahead of his pursuers—friends, concerned citizens and well-wishers alike. Mimosas on the beach. A pint in the shadow of Big Ben.

I'm going to try again. Concentrate harder to find Waldo. This time, I'll work day and/or night until I get it right. And when I see him, hidden in plain sight on the beach in Rio de Janeiro, standing between a stall selling umbrellas and an overturned candy cane delivery truck, I'll pull off his silly hat and those black glasses and I'll embrace him firmly.

"It's alright," I'll say. "You can come home. Your girlfriend is pregnant. You're going to be a father." And while he stands, speechless, doing math as to when he last saw his lost love, I'll slip on his disguise and fade into the pages, disappearing in a crowd at an Ohio State football game or in the Mall of America. I'll let anonymity wash over me and begin a game of my own. Peanut butter and jelly on the Riviera, a Coke at the Kremlin.

The Monster Hunter's Apprentice Writes Home

I told my mother I'm fine. She frets if she doesn't hear from me. The letter reads like a message home from some summer camp in the woods. Camp Killamonster sounds appropriate, I guess.

For craft time today, we made lanyards and painted ashtrays. And burned demons in the lake. I'm getting good at archery, running and screaming. I drink a lot of water, just like you told me. I wear sunscreen and bug repellant. Just like you told me. The councilor says I'm a natural fisherman, and I make good bait. I drew a picture of the sunset over the docks. It's not the best; some beast kept rising from the water and blocking the view. Still, I think Mom will like it.

Really, it's a few dull sentences. I'd rather she didn't know what happens out here. It would make her anxious. I don't want her to be anxious. She thinks we're visiting famous baseball parks around the country. In the letter, I tell her we have just visited Fenway Park in Boston. It opened in 1912. It has never been destroyed by a giant monster, though the day is young.

The Mothra Comeback Interview

No, no. Now's fine. It's good. Come in. I was just up late, that's all. Damn neighbor left his porch light on all night. I was smacking myself up against it until about four this morning. Need my beauty rest, you know?

Are you recording? Good. Let me be honest with you. It's all true. Every word. I had it all—fame, money. Silk. And women? You know about the twins, right?

Hey, girls? Come in here and sing something for the man. Yeah. That's nice. Anyway, I had it and lost it, all because of my habit. What can I say, it's genetics. My people have a thing for sweaters. I was up to eight, ten cardigans a day. I started out at Macy's with the high-end stuff, then began hanging out at Burlington Coat Factory during the lean years and finally hit rock bottom rummaging through the Goodwill stores looking for discarded knits. It was awful. A real low.

But I beat it.

I'm clean now.

I'm proud to say I own the largest private collection of *Cosby Show* sweaters in the world now. Impressive, isn't it? A few years ago, I would've torn through them in no time. But now I can admire them for their aesthetic qualities; the bright yellows, the screaming blues, the neon oranges…

Excuse me for a moment. Girls? Take five please. I'm talking here. Maybe head poolside? Thanks.

Godzilla? Screw Godzilla. There. I said it. Was he at my intervention? NO. Come see me in rehab? Nope. He was off working on that God-awful

American movie of his. Did you see that one? Who's he trying to fool? He obviously had some work done. A facelift, minimum, probably a tummy tuck as well.

I'm glad the film tanked. I really am.

And this new one? Well, someone's become a bit of a drama queen, haven't they?

What have I been doing lately? Some character work—plays mostly. Did you catch my Guildenstern at the Boise Dinner Theater? No? The critics said I really stood out. And my Tevye in *Fiddler* truly brought down the house. I've been keeping busy. I had a few meetings with the *Cloverfield* people, but that one didn't pan out. I was in an episode of *Law & Order* once, but my scene got cut in post-production.

Pardon. Someone want to close that window? I can still hear them singing out there. Thanks.

I'm sorry, this is embarrassing, but I must know... Those are really nice socks, are they wool or is that a blend?

My Zombie Journal

Day 1
This isn't so
bad. Took me forever
to walk to the
Post Office, though.
Wish I were one
of those fast zombies
like in the movies.

I wonder if that
guy on the lawn
is dead or sleeping?

Day 2
Turns out the guy
on the lawn
was dead. Too bad.
So hungry. Wandered along
with some other
zombies toward
the mall for a while.

Seemed like
a stupid idea. Who would
hide at the mall?

Day 3
Down brains the river

I brains some
people hiding on a
boat. They waved and
taunted me with
their brains. Mmmm.
Sea food.

Sadly, I
discovered I can't
swim anymore.

Brains 5
Brains in brains
brains
brains brains the brains
others won't
share brains
with the brains
of us.

Stupid brains
making me
brains even more.

Day 6
Floated into
a city filled
with brains.
Some guy shot me
twice. I ate him.
It was great. Not so
hungry anymore.

I think better on
a full stomach.

Day 21
I know I had
two
arms when I came
into this town
But I seem
to have left one
somewhere.

Ah well,
dude with the
chainsaw was tasty.

Day 28
Started walking
down the highway
toward the capitol.
Ran into a
group of zombies all
chanting
"Spleens, Spleens."

You really
find some weirdos out
in the suburbs.

Nanobots, Leeches, Salves and Lasers

To crawl inside your wounds
to eat what's within,

Replace it all with replicas
and dopplegangers,
connect the tissue with sinewy
fibers made somewhere offshore.
Drop in smart parts,
snips and snails,
things grown on lab rats
and guinea pigs

Thump, thumping sounds
turn into *click, clacks, tick, tocks.*

Would an old-fashioned
movie projector fit in there?
Could your life be hand-threaded
among the reels
to share your life as it flashes past
and rewind
to your favorite bits
over and again?

When the time comes,
could a tiny Hadron Collider
be implanted in your shell
so we could see the origin

of your universe;
view the moment where the nothing
became something and the something
became you?

Notes on Ordering a Deathbot by Mail

It is always
difficult
to say the least
with interchangeable arms
to get the combination
just right.

Machine gun
for left limb,
flamethrower
for right?

The claw is probably
the toughest
decision by far.
It is the least
destructive and yet
most versatile choice.

Buzzsaw
on one side,
laser
on the other?

The worst part
about ordering
is the appalling
lack of colors available
to the consumer.
Silver, gray, gold maybe.

Never take
the bullhorn,
never take
the spotlight

Some kids save
all their lives
for a blue and red
robot with
the grenade launcher
dart gun combo

Only to be
severely let down
as adults

Nothing Out There

I can see the sunshine
as I rest on the ocean floor.
It shimmers and dances
through the water—
a tiny imp
darting among the fish

The Patchwork Monster Looks On
as the Mad Scientist Shaves Himself

So close,
the sharp thing.
One slip,
one slip,
the blood flows
and I'm free.

Persistence of Vision

A mouse digging through the field
A rusting milk can on the porch
A multicolored quilt
across the back of a couch
Home comes in bits of flaking grit
and creaks of stairs
It comes in the sudden flight of birds
at an unfamiliar approach
A slowly opened curtain
at the knock of a stranger
A methodically rising garage door
A flag standing red on a mailbox
Home is the memory of a driveway of stones

Phoenix Lander at the Loneliest Drive-Thru

A tiny beaker full of soil
cooked up in the on-board lab.
Salty, yes. But still;
an hors d'oeuvre, a snack, a somewhat Happy Meal
Just missing ice for the soda
and the planet would be civilized.

Quiet

Our time beneath the waves was marked in bubbles and currents—the crunch of angel fish feasting on coral—the distant chop of the ship's propeller—heartbeats and sighs.

Deeper down, deeper down, deeper down.

All the far away noises muted by the ocean.

Our time beneath the waves wasn't burdened by the passage of the sun or the rising of Earth's satellite. It was measured by the number of hissy reptilian respirations through a mouthpiece, the amount of air left in our tanks.

Deeper down, deeper down, deeper down.

The ocean silences the clamor and the tumult.

The Secondary Character's Revenge

Just another story about a girl who couldn't stand you
The kind of kid you overlooked in school
This wouldn't be the one you took to prom
Or the one you kissed beneath the stairs.

It's just a tale of somebody you wronged so wrongly
Yet you never even knew existed in your sphere

This is a story of horrible revenge and bloody murder
Potions dark and spells arcane
No one would sell the girl a handgun
She'd never had an aptitude for knives.

She could bake a pie like no one's business
But the physics of ballistics drove her mad

This story is about a girl who couldn't stand you
You should be used to that by now
Your callous actions, and offensive words
Have been well known since forever. Since forever.

Maybe your company put her father on the street
No food, no roof, no security
You've burned a lot of bridges
And torched a few old buildings in your day.

But she could ice a cake like you wouldn't believe
And she could read up on poisons and pills

Just another story about a girl with a special power

Not a superhero or a cop
Just a nobody with an axe to grind
And a recipe for some mean apple strudel

At that next grand opening
Or that celebration of your next big merger
Vet your caterer well or
Don't think twice about that cupcake in your hand

It'll be delicious
It'll be sweet
Like all revenge

So, I'll be Your Monster Today

I know, I know.
There's no 'Wow' factor here.
I'm the last monster on your list.
Third string at best.
But here I am.

I won't level your town, but
I can annoy the hell out of your neighbors.
Listen:
Rawrrrr.
I know, it's weak.
I'm working with a voice and movement coach.

I know, I know.
I'm not your Gamera or your Monster Zero.
But I'm trying.
Working out.
Deep squat thrusts.
Yoga.
I'm doing yoga.
There's that.
I'm getting there.

Somebody on Shore

The man on the beach is just an apparition. A trick of my mind. I see him each time we leave port bound for some Godforsaken backwater island full of gibbering locals. Though I can never see this figure's face, he is Death, assuring me I'm not beyond his reach. I'm never on dry land long enough for him to lay his icy hand at my throat, but it's only a matter of time. How does that old poem go? "Because I could not stop for death, He kindly stopped for me?" Dickenson was on to something there. Gentleman Death has stopped for me just at the shoreline. Idly passing time. With each weighing of the anchor, I find Death staring offhandedly at me and shifting yellowed beach sand from hand to hand, a massive castle half-built at his feet.

Spoiler Alert

You like to be surprised.
I know this much.
You love it when you never see it coming,
but I'm going to ruin the ending for you.

It's the third act and the gun is off the mantle.
The undead are already inside the mall.
The computer has become self-aware and
The calls are coming from inside the house.

See, the rescue party isn't coming
and the asteroid is on a collision course with Earth.
We should've cut the blue wire and not the red
The miracle cure has become the dreaded disease.

I know you like to be surprised and
you love it when you never see it coming,
but I'm afraid I'm going to have to ruin
the ending for you.

We aren't going to make it.
We're not getting out of this together.
No triumphant sunrise.
No holy water squirt guns in the nick of time.

And the monster's never dead.
The Monster Is Never Dead.

We can cover more ground if
we split up. You check the basement;

I'll explore the attic. Walk away in opposite
directions and wait
for the screen to fade to black.

Cue the hag in the
deep dark woods
trying to eat the fat kids.

Signal the inbred mutant freaks
at the roadside rest stop
looking for fresh flesh.

Let the machete-wielding maniac
know he has five minutes before
we need him on stage.

Tourist Trap

When they put the shells up to their ears,
that's when we get them. We slide
from our hiding places and strike.

Hear the ocean?
Nope. That's merely the sound of us
sweeping down the ear canal.
From there, it's easy to wire ourselves
directly into the brain, control everything.

We started small, so as not to alarm them.
Forced them to wear black socks with sandals.
Made them crisp their skin in the mid-day sun.
Simple stuff.

We're getting bolder though.
We've programmed them to come back
every year to this same patch of sand
so we can feed on them again.

After that, who knows?
The world is our oyster,
metaphorically speaking.

UFOs Over Toledo Spell Out Dirty Word

A filthy word, a horrible word.
One so heinous that newspapers couldn't print it
without asterisks in place of some letters
but unedited photos made it around the Internet
faster than anyone could've imagined.

The guessing and theorizing began immediately
as to what they meant by it

The popular idea on the Web
was the suggestion that the aliens
thought we should have more sex.

The only disagreement was about why.
One camp thought they wanted our population to expand
so they had more humans to enslave, or eat.
Another group believed they were trying
to save the world by suggesting we needed more people
to fight off an impending attack by other aliens.

Some military specialists suggested
it wasn't a curse word at all
rather a highly advanced tactical formation
that made perfect military sense
if the craft were invading.

The government initially chalked it up to
swamp gas, then weather balloons
and the Northern Lights.

A vocal minority thought it was an expression
of disappointment.
Like a twelve-year-old setting foot
in the Magic Kingdom for the first time.

Watching Monster Snuff Films with Old Man Van Helsing

He owns an original print
of a vampire getting
his due.
It's not clean and easy
like in Hollywood
There is blood.
Gallons of it.
Pleading, begging.
There are screams of agony.

He's shown his werewolf
clip to a select few.
A terrified hunter takes
a half dozen ineffectual shots at
the thing
before a well-prepared
creature killer
puts a silver bullet
in the thing's cranium.

There's never satisfaction
on his face as he watches.
He never
looks away.
When he speaks of them,
it is with sadness, loss—
Not at the destruction
of the beasts, but regret
at the missed opportunity.

Chances that will
never
come again.

What a Wealth of Knowledge

Occipital lobe.

Occipital lobe.

It's one of those words or phrases that lose all meaning when you say it over and over.

Occipital lobe.

Occipital lobe.

Like Sheboygan and metamorphosis. Fun to say, but they're pretty much gobbledygook after a while.

Sheboygan.

Sheboygan.

It's fun, try it, you'll see.

MetamorphosisMetamorphosisMetamorhposis.

Am I wrong?

How about Chupacabra?

Chupacabra. Chupacabra.

We shout it daily. Multiple times daily, but after a while, it sounds like mush.

Look out for that Chupacabra. Your Chupacabra looks sad.

The Chupacabra has a terrible backswing.

ChupacabraChupacabraChupacabra.

See what I mean?

Help us Occipital Lobe. Sheboygan will Chupacabra them.

Metamorphosis. Metamorphosis, Metamorphosis.

What in Neptune's Name?

In the night, a drip, drip, drip
keeps me awake.
It might be a leak of some importance,
to this ship,
or it could just be the ocean
playing tricks on me.

I want to rest. Tomorrow's fresh horror
requires my full attention.
but I can't shut my eyes.
That's when I see yesterday's beasts.

When sleep comes, the dreams of flames
are more frequent
and this phoenix must surely be my doom.
Even in sleep, the heat becomes unbearable.
Surrounded by water, do the flames stand
a chance?
Drip.

Will the sea douse the fiery hell and spare
me, or will that bird
carry me off to some reward?

What WAS that thing?

There are bees buzzing in my head, my blood.
Hornets.
I can't keep myself still from all the excitement.
Nobody else hears that?
One cricket, a thousand crickets?
I need to get them out, make them quiet.
My limbs are numb from the power,
the energy, the sheer enormity
of this cosmos raging in my heart.

Worse Than it Looks, I'm Afraid

A volcanic mess?
The whole island is sinking?
Who can help me now?

You Will be Visited by Three Ghosts

In a newly-remodeled TGI Fridays
Jim Morrison's ghost materialized,
knocked my spinach dip
to the tile floor,
screamed
"Mother? I'm going to kill you."
Right in my
Face.
So rude.
His shirtless torso shimmered sweaty
in the family-friendly lighting.

At the office
the day of the big presentation
Jimi Hendrix wedged himself
into my tiny cube
produced a zippo,
some lighter fluid.
Set a Stratocaster ablaze.
My project was singed.
My meeting ruined.
I was passed over for promotion
three days later.

On the throughway,
rush hour traffic stalled.
Janis Joplin flashed past
in the car pool lane, driving
a Hummer.
A bottle of Jack shattered

on my windshield as she went.
A bumper sticker read 'My other
car is a Mercedes'.

I awoke in the night,
a gravelly voice whispering,
elaborating on my failures,
counting crimes against
my younger self.
I opened my eyes to
the sight of such a horrid
specter sitting on my bed,
I had to squeeze them
shut again.
Groggy and disoriented,
it took my addled
mind a minute to sort out
whether Keith Richards
was actually dead or alive.

The Great Zombie Pyramid Scheme

The toughest part
is convincing those first
two people.

After that, everyone
is more than happy
to bite their friends.

Credits

The Long-Term Effects of Auroral Kilometric Radiation on the Earth's Population originally appeared in *Astropoetica*.

Footnotes are the New Titles originally appeared in *Sunspinner*.

The Golden Age of Railroad Advertising first appeared in *Midwest Literary Magazine*.

The Ghost of a Beloved Children's Show Host appeared in *Illumen*.

Ideal Childhood appeared in *inkburns*.

Maybe Waldo Had Syphilis appeared in *Tigershark*.

Mothra Comeback Interview came in second in the Odysseycon annual prose poem contest for 2010 and appeared on their site.

My Zombie Journal appeared in *Vicious Verses and Reanimated Rhymes* (and was featured in a New York Times article on zombie poetry).

Notes on Ordering a Deathbot by Mail appeared in *Escape Clause*.

Persistence of Vision appeared in *inkburns*.

Tourist Trap appeared in *Silver Blade Magazine*.

Watching Monster Snuff Films with Old Man Van Helsing appeared in *House of Horror*.

You Will Be Visited By Three Ghosts appeared in *Ghostlight*.

Zombie Pyramid Scheme appeared in *Dreams & Nightmares*.

Author Bio

Matt Betts has a very real problem. His pop culture addiction to bad movies, 80s cartoons, and cheesy horror is getting way out of hand. Do not approach him with comic books, whatever you do. Traces of it can be found throughout his steampunk adventure novel *Odd Men Out* and urban fantasy *Indelible Ink*, both available from Dog Star Books. Matt's poetry was previously collected in *See No Evil, Say No Evil*. His work also appears in numerous journals, websites, magazines and anthologies.

If anyone asks, he was with you last Thursday. All night. Thanks.

Matt lives in Columbus, Ohio with his wife and sons.

www.ingramcontent.com/pod-product-compliance
Lightning Source LLC
Chambersburg PA
CBHW030355180626
46812CB00007B/2898